# BEETHOVEN

## DANCES FOR THE PIANO

*(19 Short Pieces to Play Before His Sonatinas)*

### EDITED BY MAURICE HINSON

AN ALFRED MASTERWORK EDITION

 Alfred

Second Edition
Copyright © MMII by Alfred Music Publishing Co., Inc.
All rights reserved. Printed in USA.

ISBN-10: 0-7390-2730-1
ISBN-13: 978-0-7390-2730-1

*Cover art:* The Old Burgtheater in Vienna, *1783*
*by Carl Schütz (Austrian, 1745–1800)*
*Colored etching*
*Historisches Museum Stadt Wien, Vienna, Austria*
*Erich Lessing/Art Resource, New York*

# CONTENTS

*This edition is dedicated to Frances Burnett*
*with much appreciation and admiration.*

# FOREWORD

Ludwig van Beethoven (1770-1827) composed dances from his early days through his late career. He lived during the time when the *minuet* was highly cultivated, and from 1792 on in the city of Vienna, that became a center of dance music. Vienna, the great musical city of Mozart and Haydn, immediately captured Beethoven's affection on his arrival. There he remained for the rest of his life. By 1796, Beethoven was enjoying one of the happiest periods in his life. During this time he was in great demand as a pianist. He was popular with many rich and influential families and frequently played many of the dances in this collection at afternoon garden and evening parties.

Some of the dances that were popular in Vienna at this time were vigorous *ecossaise* and the soft swaying *Ländler*, which soon changed into the most famous dance of all times, the *waltz*. Beethoven composed a large quantity of dances for practical use which were written over a long period of years for a variety of purposes and which were even occasionally incorporated into larger works. His interest in dance music can be seen specifically in his Sixth Symphony, and he used the tune of *Country Dance* WoO 14, No. 7 in the Finale of the Eroica Symphony. He composed true *Gebrauchsmusik* (Utilitarian music) for all types of festive occasions and wrote a number of marches, polonaises, and ecossaises for military band (WoO 18-24) as well as numerous dances for the piano. A march in D major was written for Archduke Anton as commander of the *Hoch-und-Deutschmeister* Regiment. It became very popular during the War of Liberation under the name of "Yorkscher Marsch" (after the Prussian general Yorck). The heroic element, symbolized in signal and march motives definitely connected Beethoven with the music of the French Revolution. Sketches for the "Yorkscher Marsch" are found together with those for the Piano Concerto Op. 73 (the "Emperor"). This "heroic work" contains a number of march motives. Sketched concurrently, the march and the concerto share some of the same elements.

Besides these military marches, Beethoven wrote over one hundred *ecossaises*, minuets, German Dances, *Ländler*, Country dances (WoO 3, 7-17), and waltzes. Most were intended for balls, name-day celebrations, and festivities. Some are still available in their original form for orchestra, some in the then popular form of trio arrangement for two violins and bass, and many in his own piano reductions. The charming *Six Ecossaisen* (WoO 83), which is in an unknown hand, are probably also piano transcriptions.

More use should be made of these small forms in teaching, recitals, and home use, and this fact is one of the main reasons for presenting this collection. These dances prove that Beethoven was not all the time the "hero," the "Titan," the "heaven stormer," as he is commonly represented. That this was not so is shown by the circumstances surrounding the composition of one of his sets of dances, the *Mödlinger Tänze* (WoO 17) for seven string and wind instruments, composed in the summer of 1819. At the time Beethoven lived in Mödling, a surburb of Vienna, and was busy composing the great Missa Solemnis. A group of musicians playing at a neighborhood inn urgently begged him for a set of waltzes. He obliged with these dances, writing out the instrumental parts himself.

Beethoven's dances are so appealing, straightforward in their rhythmic construction and charming in their harmonic and melodic design, that they serve as a perfect introduction to his seven sonatinas. These dances may be played in groups or singly. They never fail to captivate an audience.

# DEFINITIONS OF THE DANCE FORMS

### ALLEMANDE

This is a Peasant dance still in use in parts of Germany and Switzerland. It is in triple time, and of waltz-like character. Occasionally, composers have called a composition of this type a *Deutscher Tanz* (plural, *Deutsche Tänze*), or simply *Deutsch* (plural, *Deutsche*).

### COUNTRY DANCE

*Contredanse* (Fr.), *Contradanza* (It.) *Kontretanz* (Ger.). This type of dance is of British origin. Its various foreign names have come about from a plausible false etymology ("counger-dance")—one in which the performers stand opposite one another—as distinguished from a round dance. Both Mozart and Beethoven wrote Country Dances (*Kontretanze*). Number seven of Beethoven's 12 *Kontretanze* contains a theme used also in the finale of the *Eroica* Symphony and other works. The term is generic, and covers a whole series of figure dances deriving from the amusements of the English village green. Such dances became popular at the Court of Queen Elizabeth I, and during the Commonwealth were systematically described by Playford in his *English Dancing Master*. In the early years of the nineteenth century, the *Waltze Quadrille* drove the Country Dance out of the English ballroom; the folk dance of the twentieth century has brought it into considerable use again. Scotland has retained a number of its country dances throughout its history.

### ECOSSAISE

A type of contredanse in duple time. The origin of the name is a mystery, since there appears to be nothing Scottish about the character of the music. It is not the same as the *Schottische*.

### LÄNDLER

Type of slow waltz originating in the Landel, part of Austria north of the Ems river. Beethoven and Schubert composed *ländler* and the rhythm is used by Mahler in his symphonies.

### MINUET

*Menuet* (Fr.), *Minuetto* (It.), *Menuett* (Ger.). A dance in triple time, originally a French rustic dance and adapted by the court in the seventeenth century. So called because of small, dainty steps (menu = small).

### WALTZ

*Valse* (Fr.), *Walzer* (Ger.). Dance in 3/4 time probably deriving from the German *Ländler* which came into prominence in the last quarter of the eighteenth century both among composers and in the ballroom.

# THIS COLLECTION

The purpose of this collection is to provide pieces that are particularly appropriate for the intermediate student's technical and musical development. They have much audience appeal since they meet the listener on his own ground, and do not compel him to make an effort to understand what is going on. They please (by agreeable sounds and rational structure) and move (by imitating feelings), but do not astonish (by excessive elaboration) and never puzzle (by too great complexity).

These delightful dances have clear formal structure, predictable chord progressions, almost purely harmonic and homophonic texture, compact melodic style, and clearly divided melodies into antecedent and consequent, thereby making them easily understood by students who, at this stage, may not be ready to understand and approach complicated, emotional, and ambiguous artistic terminologies.

Students who understand these dances in terms of musicianship and technique may be led gradually to more complicated or unusual repertoire with ease and understanding. The dances are placed in alphabetical sequence.

# GUIDE TO PERFORMANCE PRACTICES IN THE DANCES

Each individual offers a unique interpretation of a music composition. Interpretation reflects personal taste, background, education, culture, and human artistic experience. However, interpretation should be strongly influenced by style. A fine performance should follow and project the composer's intention carefully, aside from the matter of technicality. Indeed, the main problem in interpretation is coming as close as possible to what we know to be the intentions of the composer; and from that basis, taking your own flight of imagination. Music is best served by matching our modern interpretations as closely as possible to what we believe (on historical grounds transmitted by surviving contemporary evidence) to have been the original interpretations. Therefore, interpretation is on the one hand serving the intentions of the composer and on the other hand putting the interpreter's own blood and personality into the realization of the text. These two areas must be balanced.

## I. PEDALING

Pedaling is totally dependent on critical listening and requires perfect coordination of hand and foot. For these dances, the pedal must be changed to allow for clarity of melody as well as harmony. The speed of the melody, especially, will determine the pedal application of these pieces. Longer melodic notes (quarter-note or more), against chordal or Alberti accompaniments or anything but counterpoint, can generally be pedaled. Discretely used pedaling will help recreate the spirit of Classical style.

Except for Beethoven, few composers in the Classical period gave pedal indications in the score, and even Beethoven only notated pedalings in a few compositions. Beethoven is considered a pioneer in pedal practice, but he used pedal more often than he indicated in his scores. He did not include pedal markings in these dances but numerous places need pedal and the editor has added these. There are also many passages in these pieces in which pedaling is not marked, but can be pedaled.

Listed below are a few accepted damper (right) pedaling practices that apply not only to Beethoven but to much of the piano literature from the Classical period:

1. The pedal must be changed at least as often as the harmony changes.

2. The damper pedal is used when a legato sound is desired. Slower, longer melodic notes in Classical style can be pedaled.

3. Arpeggio and broken chord passages provide opportunities for pedal use.

4. Damper pedal use is associated with dynamics. This pedal enriches the sounds through sympathetic vibration of the overtones. Beethoven frequently suggested pedaling to assist both crescendo and descrescendo.

5. The pedal may be used to increase the pungency of certain accented harmony, especially dissonant ones such as found in the *Ecossaise* in G, WoO 23 on page 18, measures 4 and 20.

6. Pedal may also be used for staccato passages. Staccato pedal is for color and effect. The hand and foot drop together and the performer must listen carefully to get the exact desired duration. Some of these dances end with an authentic cadence of short, loud chords. Use staccato pedaling at these places whenever the music demands it.

## II. ORNAMENTS

Ornaments serve to decorate the note with which they are associated, enrich the harmony, heighten melodic attractiveness, and serve as an indispensable element of expression to the style. C.P.E. Bach described them in his *Essay on the True Art of Playing Keyboard Instruments*[1] thus:

> They connect and enliven tones and impact stress and accents; they make music pleasing and awaken our close attention. Expression is heightened by them; let a piece be sad, joyful, or otherwise, and they will lend a fitting assistance. Embellishments provide opportunities for fine performance as well as much of its subject matter. They improve mediocre compositions. Without them the best melody is empty and ineffective, the clearest content clouded. (p. 79)

All ornaments stand in proportional relationship to the length of the main note, tempo, and the characteristics of the piece. Also, most ornaments notated in small grace notes belong to the following principal note.

The short appoggiature is the ornament most frequently used by Beethoven in these dances. It is to be played as a short, rapid note regardless of the duration of the principal note (C.P.E. Bach, p. 91). Frequently it appears as a small grace note with a slash ( ♪ ) in the score which is referred to as *acciaccatura* (crushed note).

## III. TEMPO

Tempo indications are frequently provided by Beethoven in these dances. Tempo is considered of primary importance in the final performance of a composition, although there are no satisfactorily defined measurements for the Italian tempo indications. The tempo at which a piece is performed may vary from one performer to another, and there is some evidence indicating that present-day performers prefer faster tempos than those of previous historical periods. There is wide latitude in determining the tempo. A good tempo at one performance may not be desirable for every performance. Beethoven was very much annoyed by his own metronome markings when he returned to reconsider them at a later date.

The editor has added metronome marks that represent an average measurement of appropriate tempo for each piece. These marks are only a general guide and a point of comparison but no more than that because they reflect only one person's judgment of the correct tempo at the specific moment.

[1]Bach, C.P.E. *Essay on the True Art of Playing Keyboard Instruments*. Translated and edited by William J. Mitchell. New York: W. W. Norton, 1949.

The Italian tempo terms indicate the mood of the musical contents. The correct tempo of any piece should be deduced from overall mood. The appropriate rate of pulse should be governed by the rhythmic organization, relative speed of the various sections, and other characteristics of the piece. A serious and weighty piece should take a slower pace than a playful and dance-like piece. Unity of tempo is more important in the Classical era than in later periods. C.P.E. Bach generalized tempo indications in his *Essay* as follows:

> The pace of a composition, which is usually indicated by several well-known Italian expressions, is based on its general content as well as on the fastest notes and passages contained in it. Due consideration of these factors will prevent an allegro from being rushed and an adagio being dragged. (p. 151)

Intelligent use of the available musical clues from notation is an important consideration in determining the tempo. The proper tempo is the one which takes all musical and technical considerations into account.

One of the typical characteristics of these dances lies in their fairly strict tempo. No matter what tempo a performer decides, he should keep the same basic pace throughout the dance. The tempo at the end of the piece should be approximately the same as at the beginning (C.P.E. Bach, p. 161).

Yet, absolutely strict tempo is mechanical and usually is not musically satisfying. Music, and especially dance music, demands a certain degree of flexibility. The musical pulse is similar to the human pulse. If a person is happy, sad, tired, or excited, the pulse varies to a certain degree. However, both musical and human pulse cannot deviate too much from steadiness. The basic pulse of the music should be maintained because it serves as a basis for rhythmic flexibility.

This flexibility is referred to as *rubato*. Manipulating this musical pulse (*rubato*) is considered one of the highly sophisticated ways of interpreting music and it should be taught as early as possible.

## IV. DYNAMICS

Beethoven included more details of expression (i.e., dynamics, tempo indications) desired from the performer than any other earlier composer.

Dynamics may be varied by the performer according to his personal taste and the general acoustical conditions. Since there are no absolute standards for dynamics, the exact degree of loudness is usually left to the discretion of the individual performer. This discretion makes the same piece as performed by different artists appear different and thus gives a new interpretation. The various degrees of individual dynamic concept should be adjusted proportionally to the dimensions of the dances. A few dynamics have been added by the editor to help clarify musical ideas.

## V. ARTICULATION

Articulation denotes all of those factors other than dynamics contributing to the meaningful shaping of melody. It includes the areas of correct breathing, phrasing, attack, legato, and staccato. Good articulation involves the separation of the continuous melodic line into logical small units, with accentuation, dynamic rise and fall, and rhythmic acceleration and retardation as people do in speech. However, Beethoven frequently did not indicate articulation and phrasing. The editor has reconstructed much of this area in these dances according to his musical insight, experience, and knowledge.

In practice, the pianist should determine the climax and the end of a phrase according to his interpretation. A good way of making a judgment is to sing the melody. C.P.E. Bach in his *Essay* stated:

> Indeed, it is a good practice to sing instrumental melodies in order to reach an understanding of their correct performance. This way of learning is of far greater value than the reading of voluminous tomes or listening to learned discourses. In these one meets such terms as Nature, Taste, Song, and Melody, although their authors are often incapable of putting together as many as two natural, tasteful, singing melodic tones, for they dispense their alms and endowments with a completely unhappy arbitrariness. (p. 152)

Beethoven frequently uses short slurs between two notes, which are known as couplets. The proper execution of couplets requires the last note to be slightly shorter than its normal duration. The beginning note of each couplet is stressed slightly for articulation.

*Country Dance* WoO 11, No. 6
bar 9 (page 16)

Works without opus number (WoO) are numbered in accordance with Georg Kinsky, *Das Werk Beethovens, thematisch-bibliographisches Verzeichnis seiner sämtlichen vollendeten Kompositionen*, completed by Hans Halm, Munich: G. Henle Verlag, 1955. *Anhang* refers to the appendix of this book.

**Maurice Hinson**

Ludwig van Beethoven in 1802.
From a miniature painted on ivory by Hornemann.
*Courtesy of the Beethoven-Haus, Bonn.*

Oil portrait of Beethoven
by W.J. Mahler (1804).

# *LUDWIG VAN BEETHOVEN*
## *(1770–1827)*

# Allemande

WoO 8, No. 8

*D.C. al Fine*

# Allemande

WoO 81

c.1800

The autograph sketch (SG. 631) is located in Bonn, at the Beethoven-Haus.

D.C.

# Country Dance

WoO 14, No. 1

# Country Dance

WoO 14, No. 4

## Country Dance*

Allegretto ♩ = c.100

WoO 14, No. 7

* Beethoven used this theme in the Finale of the Eroica Symphony, in the 15 Variations and Fugue Op.35, and for the Ballet "The Creatures of Prometheus."

# Seven Country Dances

WoO 11
1798

**1**

**2**

3

# 4

# 5

# 6

# 7

# Ecossaise

WoO 23

# 6 Ecossaises*

WoO 83
c.1806

*Thematic unity requires these six ecossaises to be played as a group.

# Twelve German Dances

WoO 13

c.1797

*D.C. al Fine*

4

Fine

TRIO

D.C. al Fine

D.C. al Fine

**6**

*f*  *sf*  *sf*

⑨  *sf*  *sf*

*Fine*

**TRIO**  ⑰

*p*  *pp*

㉒  *p*  *sf*

㉗  *sf*  *mp*

*D.C. al Fine*

D.C. al Fine

Fine

D.C. al Fine

34

*Subito Coda*

# German Dance

**WoO 42, No. 6**
c.1795

# Ländler

Poco allegro ♩. = 63

# Ländler

WoO 17, No. 6

# Minuet

WoO 10, No. 1
1795

Minuet D.C.

# Minuet

WoO 10, No. 2
1795

*Minuet D.C.*

# Minuet

WoO 10, No. 4
1795

*Minuet D.C.*

# Waltz

Anhang 14, No. 2

# Waltz

**WoO 85**
14 Nov. 1825

Autograph: Bonn, Beethoven-Haus, SG.585

# Viennese Waltz

WoO 17, No. 3

# Viennese Waltz

WoO 17, No. 10

Allegretto ♩ = c.132